My Name Is

BOOMER!

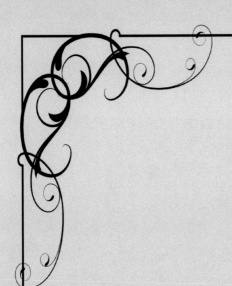

My name is Boomer

But for a long time I didn't have a name.

This is my story.

I was born under a house with brothers and sisters. We had a mommy who took care of us and fed us. Mommy loved us and she made me feel safe and secure.

But one day she left us.

We waited and waited but she never came back. Where was our mommy? We were all very sad... and soon very hungry!

We got so hungry that one by one

we crawled out from under the house

to look for food and water.

We didn't know where we were going

so we all went different ways.

I never saw my brothers and sisters

ever again.

It was hard for me to find food.

I was hungry all the time.

I found a park where people would

sometimes leave food on the ground.

But there were other dogs in the park

just like me who were hungry too.

Sometimes we would fight over food.

I didn't want to fight but I was so hungry!

When it got cold and rainy I always

crawled under a house like the place

I was born. But many nights it was very cold

and I would shake and shake until I fell asleep.

I dreamed about my mommy back when

I felt safe and secure.

Would anybody ever love me again?

I was so sad I cried a lot,

sometimes all night long.

After a while I started to feel sick.

I coughed a lot and didn't feel like

looking for food. But one day I got so hungry

I went out to find something to eat.

It was cold and raining and I was feeling

very bad. I found myself at a very busy

street corner with no food around,

but I was too cold and hungry

and sick to leave. Then it started

to rain.

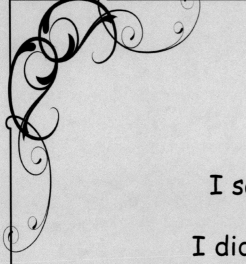

I sat down to rest and

I didn't know what to do.

Then I saw a man across the street

looking at me. I looked away then

looked at him again.

He was still looking at me.

He started walking towards me. I wanted to run

away but I was so weak I couldn't move.

He stood in front of me, bent down and petted

my head. I didn't know what to do.

Before I knew it he picked me up!

I was really scared but didn't try to get away.

He carried me across the street and put

me in his car. I had run away from cars

on the street my whole life but never thought

I would ever be inside one! It was dry and warm

so I decided I liked cars.

He stopped the car and carried me

into a building. There were other dogs

and cats with other people sitting

in a big room. A lady behind the desk

saw us come in and took us into a smaller room.

Soon a person came in who was a doggie doctor.

She looked me all over, looked in my mouth

and then stuck me with a needle.

It hurt a little but I was ok.

The man put me on a leash and walked me back to the car. We rode for a while and then got to a house. He walked me inside. It was so nice and warm! I sat on the kitchen floor wondering what would happen next. The man put a bowl of clean water and some food in front of me.

I was so happy!

I ate and drank until I couldn't eat or drink anymore.

I felt so much better, I was dry

and warm and my tummy was full,

but I was still coughing. I was very sick.

The man put some towels down on the floor

for me to sleep on. It was the most

comfortable I had ever been in my life!

I felt warm and safe like I did with

my mommy.

In the morning the man took me back to the doggie doctor. She said I was very, very sick and if the man took me to a shelter they would help me sleep forever. I didn't like the sound of that and neither did the man. So the doctor gave me a shot that really hurt! Then she gave the man some medicine for me and we went back to the house. He gave me more food and water, but I didn't want any. I just wanted to sleep.

I woke up the next morning wondering

what would happen next. Would I be

back on the street? I was still very sick

but if he got rid of me at least I had a little bit

of kindness. I could live on the street again

and I would always have the memory

of the man being nice to me and the warm house

and the food.

Just then the man came in, scratched my head and said "Boomer". He kept saying Boomer. He took me for a walk and he kept saying Boomer. When we got back to the house he said Boomer. I looked up at him. Could it be? If I have a name he's not going to put me out in the street. Could it be I have a home? I have a name! My name is Boomer!

The man sat in a chair, slapped his leg

and said my name Boomer. I jumped in his lap

and he gave me a hug and didn't let go.

I never felt so good! So safe and secure!

I have a home and someone who loves me!

I decided I was the luckiest dog in the

whole world!

A year has passed and my cough is gone

and I feel great! The doggie doctor

says my heart is ok and I'm healthy as can be.

That's wonderful but the best part

of my new life is having someone who loves me,

and I love him back.

And I love my name.

My name is Boomer!

Author Bob Kochman with Boomer

Made in the USA
Middletown, DE
09 November 2020